THE AMAZING ADVENTURES OF  LLIE

Ellie's First Plane Ride

Co-Author and Assistant Photographer - Elle Fair
Co-Author and Photographer - Marci Fair
Assistant Editor - Chloe Fair
Cover and Layout Designer - Cornelia G. Murariu

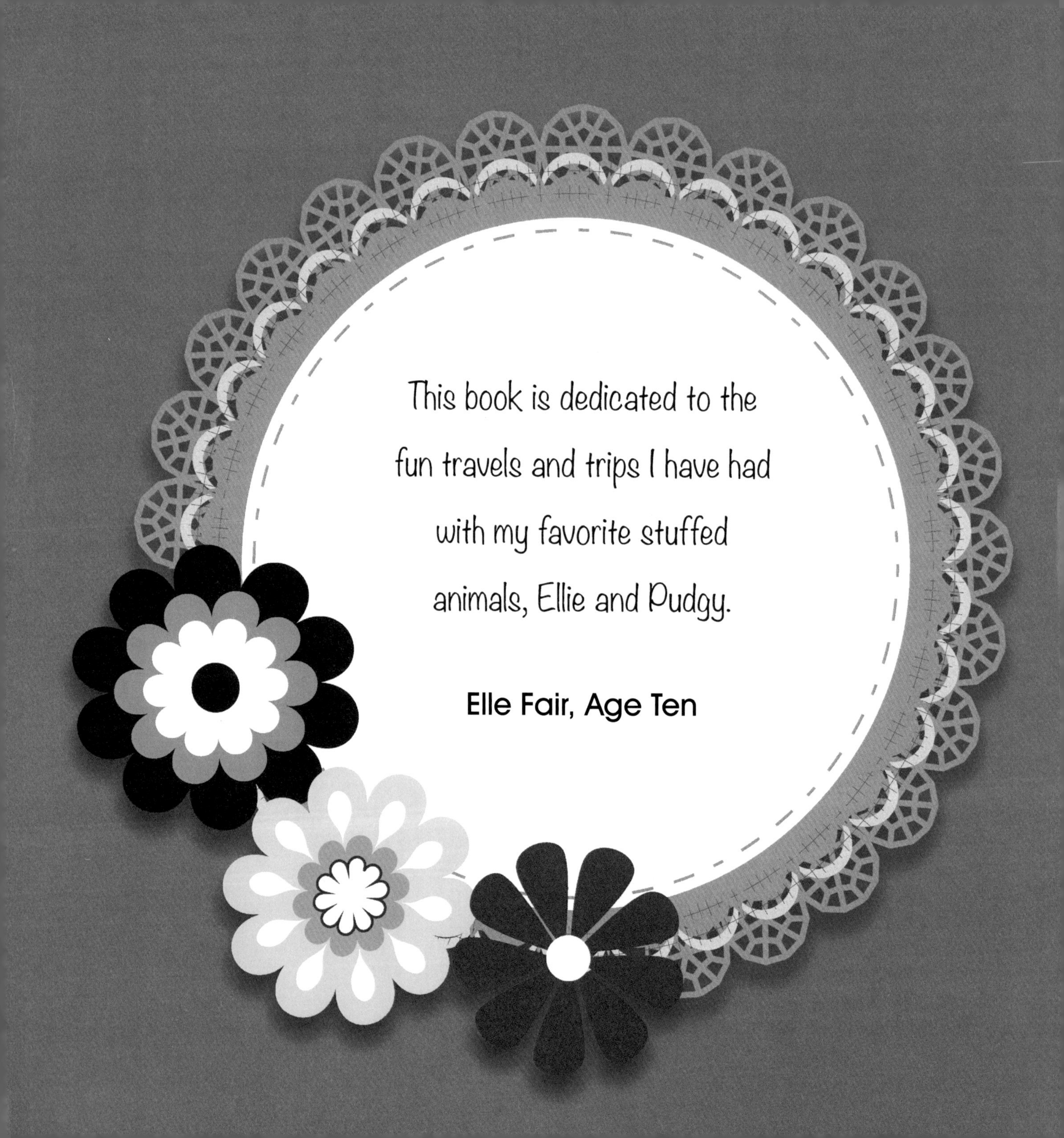

This book is dedicated to the fun travels and trips I have had with my favorite stuffed animals, Ellie and Pudgy.

Elle Fair, Age Ten

Ellie was flying to meet her faraway relatives. Her best friend, Pudgy, was coming with her. When they arrived at the airport, they checked into their flight. Ellie was nervous, but Pudgy liked to fly. She told Ellie about all the fun they would have together.

They checked to be sure their flight was leaving on time.

Wow, there were a lot of planes coming and going!

Then they rode the escalator upstairs.

Ellie was a little bit worried about the strange disappearing stairs, so Pudgy helped her. Ellie held on, and it was a fun ride up to the top.

Ellie did not know what to think about the big security machines, so she and Pudgy cuddled together in a backpack as they went through.

Whew! Since they had not worn any shoes or jewelry, it was easy. They made it through with no problems at all.

It seemed so far to their gate...

They decided to ride the tram to get there.

They found a window seat on the tram.
The ride was fast and exciting!

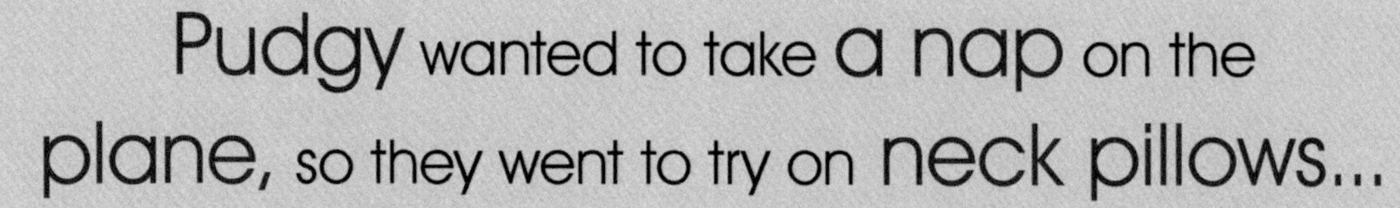

Pudgy wanted to take a nap on the plane, so they went to try on neck pillows...

...but, the pillows were just a little too big to fit them.

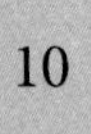

Then it was already time to board.
They found their seat and watched as suitcase
after suitcase was loaded on the plane.

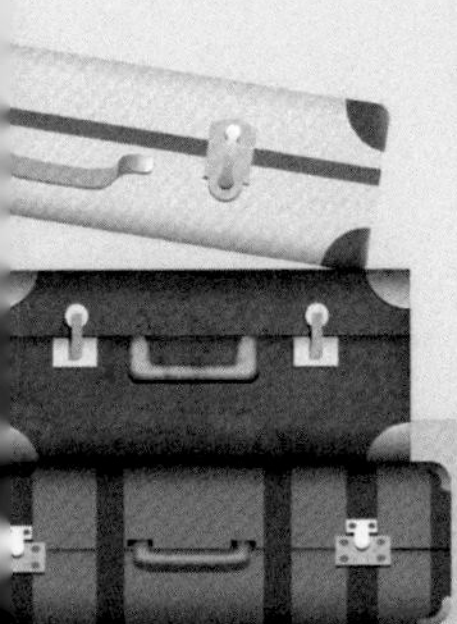

Then...liftoff!!

They were on their way.

After landing at the airport,
Ellie thought maybe
they should rent a cart to help
them with their luggage.
NOTICE
CAUTION

Next, they rode in a taxi to their hotel.
The hallway to their room seemed so long!

They finally found their room.

It had been a long, exciting day. Everything Ellie was worried about had turned out to be fine. Pudgy was a good friend.

They were very tired and ready to go to bed. Ellie fell asleep, dreaming about visiting her family the next day.

The next morning, the Big Day had arrived! They went to the zoo to meet some of Ellie's relatives.

They looked at the map. The zoo was so big, it was not going to be easy to find them.

Neither did
the Okapi
forest giraffe.

Ellie asked the Eastern Giant Eland, who told her she did not know. She said elephants were too big for her to play with anyway.

Ellie and Pudgy found lots of elephants around the zoo who looked friendly...

...but none of them had
much to say about
her real relatives.

They saw the Nyala antelopes, and met a new antelope baby named Ruby.

Pudgy gave Ellie a lift so she could see over the bushes. They saw very tall giraffes, but still no elephants.

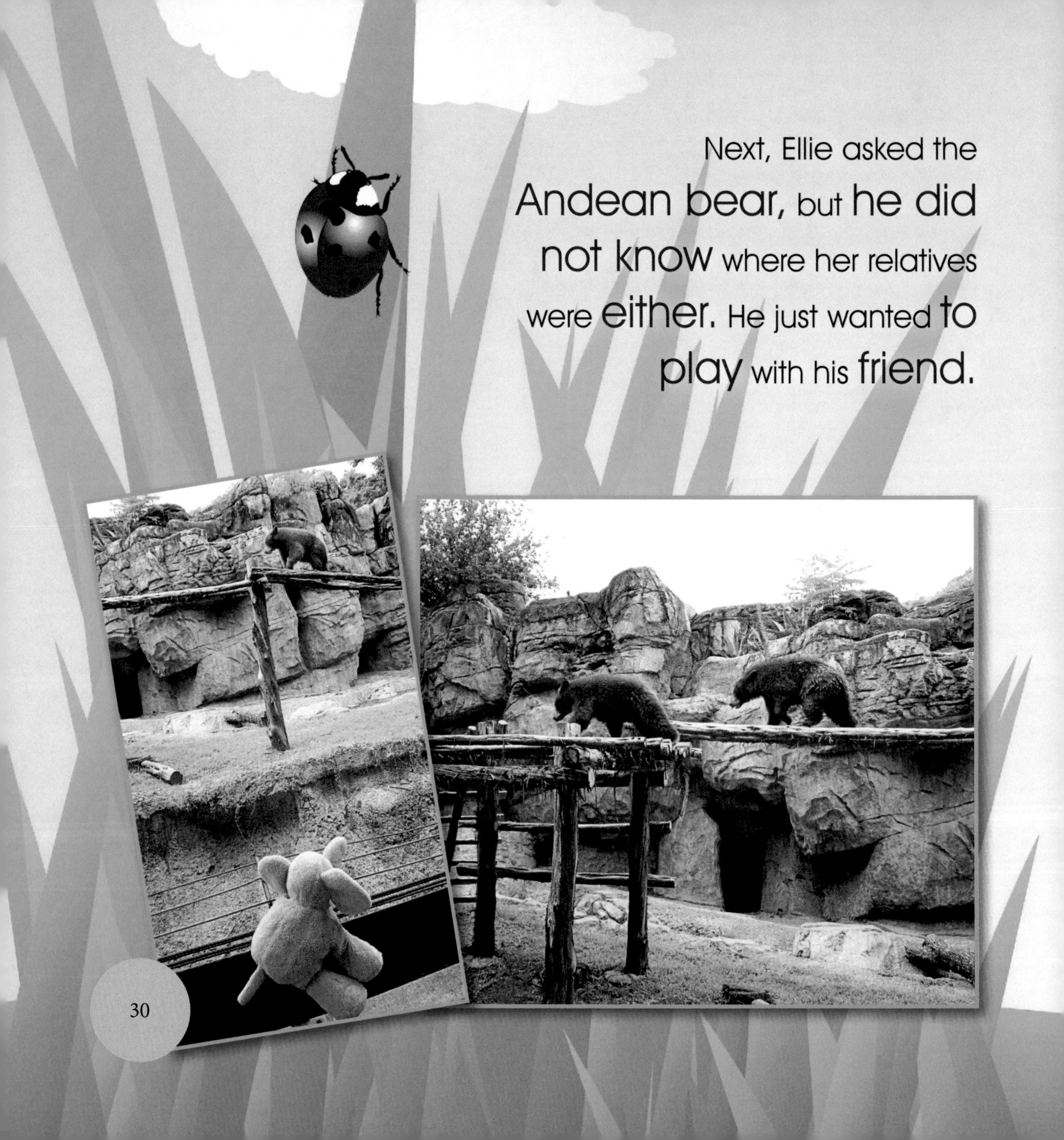

Next, Ellie asked the Andean bear, but he did not know where her relatives were either. He just wanted to play with his friend.

Ellie and Pudgy met the Baird's tapir. She was too busy swimming to talk about where to find the elephants.

The Pineywoods cattle was too tired to help and only wanted to take a nap.

The llamas did not know and only wanted to run around.

Ellie was worried she would never find them. Then she walked around the corner, and there they were!

She had found her aunt and
her baby cousin.

Then she walked over and saw her uncle and another cousin.

They were all excited to say hello. They decided that even though they were not quite the same size or color, or from the same town, that they liked each other anyway.

Her teenage cousin walked over, acting very cool, to say hello. She asked her what it was like to fly on a plane.

Ellie told her she felt like a bird when she was on the plane. Her cousin thought that was funny.

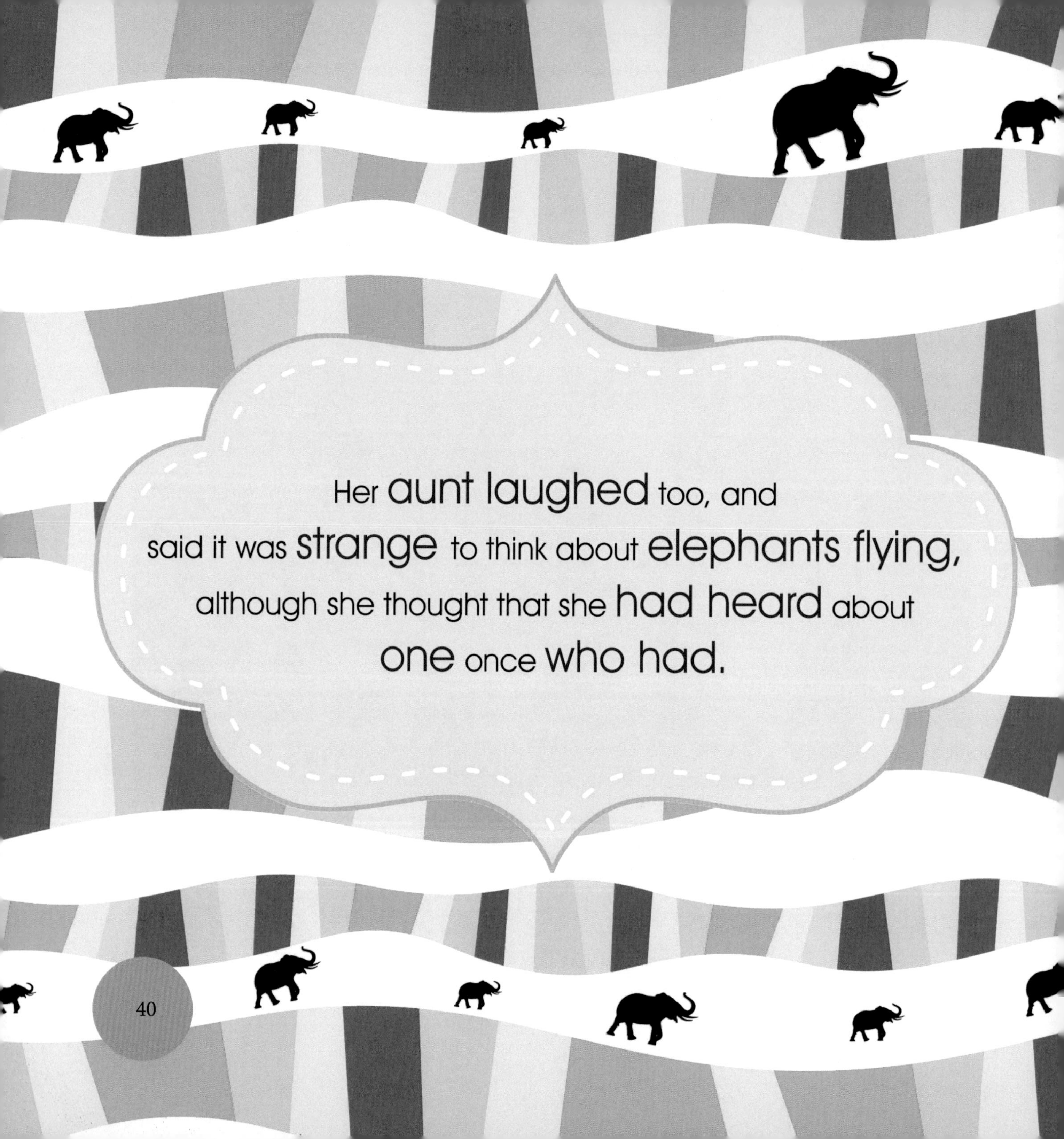

Her aunt laughed too, and said it was strange to think about elephants flying, although she thought that she had heard about one once who had.

Her baby cousin hoped that one day she would be grown up like Ellie and could fly to visit her and her friends.

It had been an amazing day. Now it was time to leave and fly back home.

Ellie did not like to say good-bye, so she just told her special relatives, "See you when I see you!"

Ellie and Pudgy went back to the airport to fly home. They were tired, so they rode the airport cart to their gate.

As they waited to board their plane, they shared fun stories from their day about all the amazing animals they met.

After they checked their luggage,
Ellie and Pudgy were happy to be safely
buckled in their seat on the plane.
It was nice to sit close together.

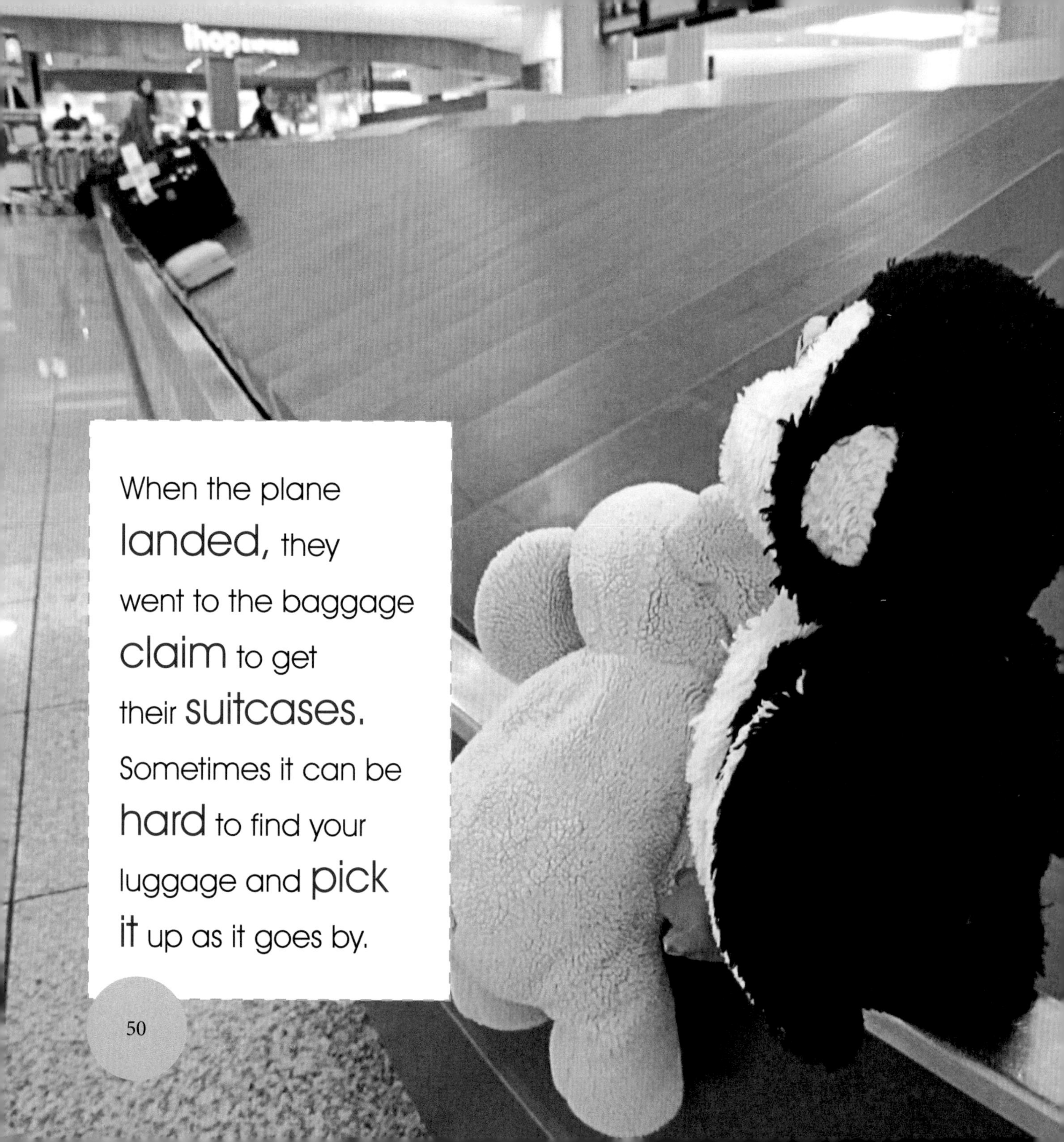

When the plane **landed,** they went to the baggage **claim** to get their **suitcases.** Sometimes it can be **hard** to find your luggage and **pick it** up as it goes by.

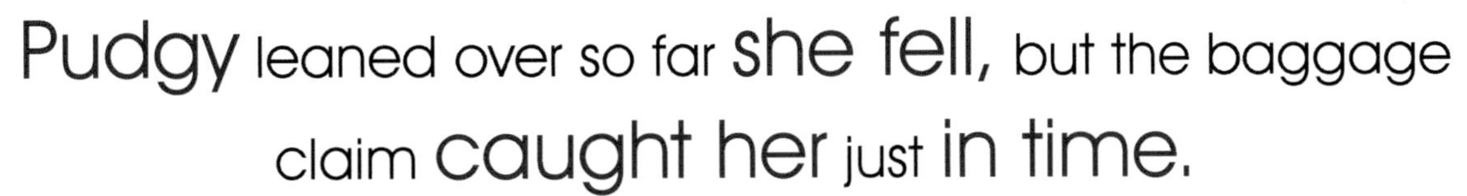

Pudgy leaned over so far she fell, but the baggage claim caught her just in time.

Then they saw their

suitcases

come around the corner.

They grabbed them
before the suitcases
could get away.

As they cuddled in bed that night,
they told their friends about all their
adventures: riding in their first airplane,
seeing all kinds of amazing animals,
meeting Ellie's very big relatives, and more!

It was a special trip together that
they would never forget.

As Ellie drifted off to sleep, she
wondered what adventure
they would have together next.

"SHARE YOUR FAVORITE STUFFED

1

Set up your favorite stuffed animals on a favorite trip or plane ride to share.

2

Take a photo or ask someone to help you take one.

WE WILL RECOGNIZE YOUR CREATIVITY AND WILL LOVE

ANIMAL FRIENDS TOO!" Here's how in four easy steps:

3

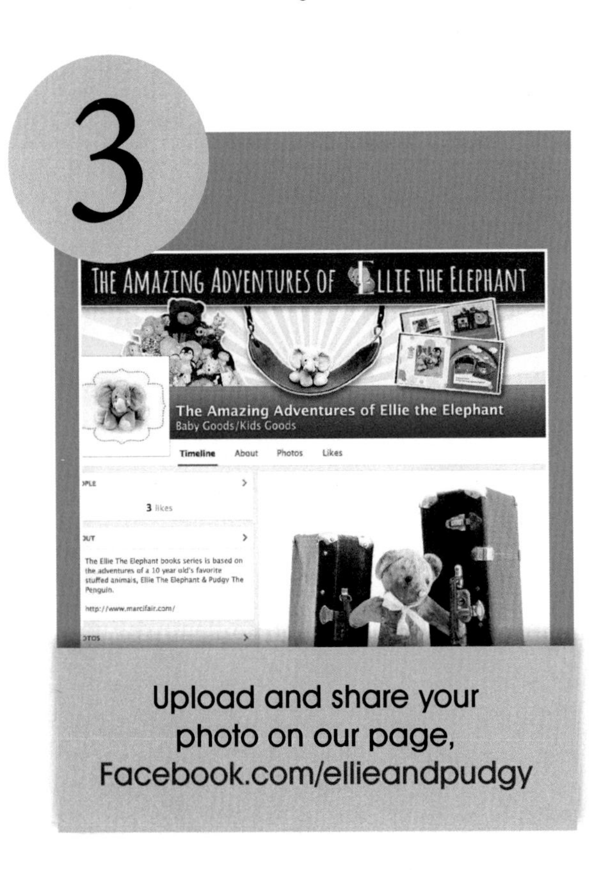

Upload and share your photo on our page, Facebook.com/ellieandpudgy

4

Tell us their names and type hashtag #elliesfriends

MEETING YOUR FAVORITE STUFFED ANIMAL FRIENDS TOO!

The Amazing Adventures of Ellie The Elephant:
Ellie's First Plane Ride

Copyright ©2014 Marci Fair, Pacochel Press LLC
All rights reserved.
First Edition

Printed in the United States of America

Permission to reproduce or transmit in any form or by any means—electronic or mechanical, including photocopying and recording—or by any information storage and retrieval system, must be obtained by contacting the author by email at info@guiltfreemom.com.

Ordering Information
For additional copies contact your favorite bookstore, online store, or email info@guiltfreemom. com. Special offers for large orders are available.

ISBN: 0692272097 ISBN 13: 978-0692272091

MORE OF ELLIE'S AMAZING ADVENTURES COMING SOON!

WWW.ELLIEADVENTURES.COM